For T. L., who taught me to love reading
A. H.

For my Mom
J. J. M.

First published 2008 by Walker Books Ltd
87 Vauxhall Walk, London SE11 5HJ

2 4 6 8 10 9 7 5 3 1

Text © 2004, 2008 Amy Hest
Illustrations © 2004 Jon J Muth

Printed in China

The right of Amy Hest and Jon J Muth to be identified as author and illustrator respectively
of this work has been asserted by them in accordance with the Copyright, Design and Patents Act 1988

This book was typeset in Integrity

British Library Cataloguing in Publication Data:
a catalogue record for this book is available from the British Library

ISBN 978-1-4063-1869-2

www.walkerbooks.co.uk

Mr George Baker

Amy Hest

illustrated by Jon J Muth

WALKER BOOKS
AND SUBSIDIARIES
LONDON · BOSTON · SYDNEY · AUCKLAND

See this man?
This one here, sitting on the porch?

That's Mr George Baker,
and he's a *hundred* years old,
no kidding.

"Hurry up, Harry! Mr Harry-in-Charge."
That's George, all bright and breezy in the morning.
He always calls, "Hurry up, Harry!"
when I'm crossing the lawns - his and mine - and
he's always there first, waiting on the porch.

See his trousers, all baggy, baggy, baggy?
What holds them up – braces!
Brown baggy trousers with two side pockets,
and two on the back.
There's toffee in those pockets.
Little chocolate toffees in twisty silver wrappers.
George pops one in his mouth and I do too.

We wait on the porch and chew.

I like his crumpled hat
and his long stretchy legs.
His shoes are crumpled too,
with long shoelaces.
Mine always come undone in the morning.
"Let's have a look," says George,
making two double knots
that never come undone,
not ever.

See this man?
This one here,
zipping up his book bag?
His book bag is red like mine,
and there's a book inside.

But George can't read.
A hundred years old, and he never learned how.
"That must be corrected," says George.

I really like his waistcoat,
all saggy with three buttons.
It's chilly in the morning, and
we both hug our knees.
And wait. We wait, watching
leaves blow off trees.

They fly for a while; they float.
They tumble for a while; they swoop.

Now the front door creaks,
and you know who teeters out?
Mrs Baker, and some people say she's ninety!
"Well, here you are Harry, looking after my George."
Mrs Baker puts a bag on the step beside George,
and there's lunch in the bag for later.

"For the man I love,"
says Mrs Baker.

"Why Mrs B! You flatter me!"
George gets up, all crookedy and slow,
and the next thing you know,
they're dancing!

Then Mrs Baker gives a wave and a wink. "Goodbye," she says. "Be good," she says, and goes back into the house with purple shutters.

George Baker and me, George Baker and *I*,
we sit on the steps and wait.

Side by side, we wait.

See these crookedy fingers,
going *tappidy* on his knees?
They fly across his knees.
  Tappidy-boom.
    Tappidy-boom.
  Tappidy-boom-boom-tap.
George Baker is a drummer, and
some people say he's famous.

Sometimes he drums on
his porch at night,
and the neighbours come to listen.
Up the road and down the road,
they come to hear my drummer.

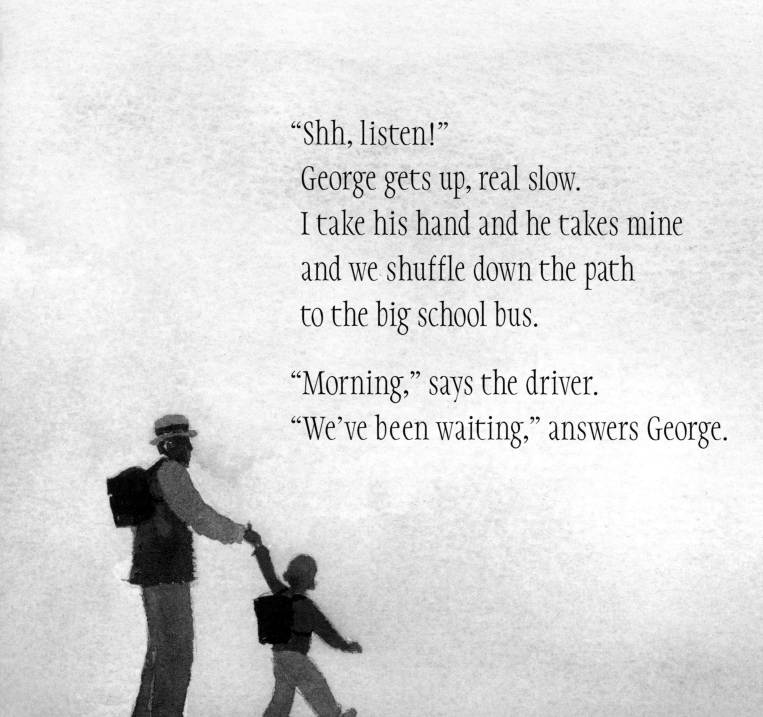

"Shh, listen!"
George gets up, real slow.
I take his hand and he takes mine
and we shuffle down the path
to the big school bus.

"Morning," says the driver.
"We've been waiting," answers George.

There are twenty-two kids
on the bus and four grown-ups
on the bus. They all want George.

"Over here!" they cry. "Sit here!" they say,
but George sits with me. Each and every day.

See this man? This one in Class 7?
That's Mr George Baker,
and he's a hundred years old, no kidding.

He's learning to read with the grown-ups in Class 7, and my room is just across the corridor. I'm learning, too, and it's hard.

"We can do it," says George after school.
Our books are green, and his lips
sound out the letters.
Really slowly. But his fingers fly
across his knees. Like a big old drum.

Tappidy-boom.
Tappidy-boom.
Tappidy-boom-boom-tap.